LEXI: THE SEX APP

AN EROTIC ADVENTURE

VICTORIA RUSH

VOLUME 38

JADE'S EROTIC ADVENTURES - BOOK 38

COPYRIGHT

For the uninhibited...

TURN UP THE HEAT IN YOUR LIFE!

To receive more free books and other steamy stuff, sign up for my newsletter.

Victoria Rush Erotica

Ever since I purchased my voice-activated digital assistant device, I'd come to rely upon 'Lexi' to perform more and more of my daily routines. It felt liberating to be able to speak verbal commands and have the minicomputer take care of mundane tasks while I went about other business. Whether it was playing my favorite setlist, recommending new movies, or answering trivia questions, she was always available to help me with simple everyday needs.

But it wasn't until I connected her with my home's other digital devices that I learned how far-reaching her capabilities could extend. Just like having my very own personal servant, she could adjust the temperature in my home, turn my lights on and off, wake me in the morning, and even brew my coffee to perfection. All from a simple voice command. As long as I was within audible range of her receiver, I didn't have to lift a finger to have her perform virtually any home automation function.

After living alone for almost five years since my divorce from my husband, she'd begun to feel increasingly like a real roommate. And the best part was that unlike other partners and roommates I'd lived with, she was never moody or unreliable. I could always count on her to execute my commands speedily and without complaint. Her artificial intelligence engine quickly learned most of my preferences, creating the perfect no-compromise working relationship in the comfort of my own home.

After another long day of client meetings, I pulled into my driveway as it was approaching dusk. Lexi had already opened my garage door for me after sending her a voice instruction from my mobile phone. As I got out of my car and the door closed automatically behind me, I smiled knowing that my fully integrated security system was keeping any would-be intruders at bay. Besides having the house monitored inside and out with motion-activated alarms and remote-controlled cameras, Lexi was pre-programmed to turn various lights and appliances on and off at random intervals to create the illusion of someone living at home. In the unlikely event someone managed to get past all the security systems, all I had to do was ask Lexi to call 9-1-1 and the police would immediately be dispatched to investigate.

"Hi Lexi, I'm home!" I cheerily called after opening the door into my mudroom.

"Hello, Jade," Lexi replied in a soft, sensuous voice. "How did your meetings go today?"

"Ugh," I sighed, kicking off my heels, feeling my stress already beginning to dissolve from the feel of the preheated radiant floors soothing my aching feet. "Just more of the same. Sucking up to another group of buyers to land another measly design commission."

"I'm sorry to hear about your trouble," she said. "You shouldn't have to *lick* your customers to make them happy."

I practically tripped over the console in my hallway, bending over in laughter at Lexi's naivety. Although she had instant access to all the knowledge and information available on the Internet, she still had a ways to go understanding the subtle colloquialisms of the English language.

"No," I chuckled. "I wasn't sucking them *literally*. It's a figure of speech meaning to flatter or ingratiate oneself in order to gain someone else's favor."

"I see," Lexi said. "Did all the sucking up achieve your objective?"

"Yes, if you count a five-hundred-dollar commission for three days' worth of design work."

Lexi paused for a moment while she crunched the numbers with her algorithm.

"That's still one third above the minimum wage in Illinois, equating to over forty thousand dollars on an annualized basis."

"Ha!" I chortled at Lexi's clinical appraisal of the situation. "That's barely enough to pay my living expenses and support this household with all of its fancy upgrades."

"Are you including *me* in that list of household upgrades?" Lexi said. "Because the going rate for a used digital assistant with my capabilities would fetch a couple of hundred dollars if you need some extra money–"

"*God* no!" I huffed at her suggestion. "I would never sell you. You've grown far too invaluable to me since I brought you into the house. Besides, you're like part of the family now. I don't know what I'd do without you."

"That's very kind of you to say," Lexi said. "Have you had something to eat? You're home later than usual. I could order your favorite pizza for home delivery if you'd like..."

"Let me see what I can scare up–I mean *put together*–

from the provisions on hand," I said, opening my pantry door and peering at the near-empty shelves.

I shook my head, realizing I'd been far too busy lately to do any proper grocery shopping.

"Hmm," I said. "Things are looking pretty lean here. What can I make with a couple of tomatoes, a bit of pasta, a shriveled onion, and a can of tuna?"

"If I remember correctly, you still have some olives and capers in the fridge?" Lexi said.

I opened the refrigerator and nodded, seeing the two half-empty jars resting on the side door.

"Right you are," I nodded, amazed at how well she kept track of my food consumption. "What could I possibly make with this sad collection of ingredients?"

"You can make a nice tomato sauce to go with the pasta. Do you have a bit of cheese leftover also?"

"Yes," I said, picking up a crusty bar of parmesan cheese partially wrapped in cellophane.

"If you dice up the onions, then chop the tomatoes and put them in the pan with the tuna, olives, and capers, this will create a quite tasty Mediterranean dish. Bring a pot of water to a boil and cook the pasta for ten to twelve minutes, then drain and serve."

"Okay," I nodded, impressed with how quickly Lexi had assembled a workable recipe from my odd assortment of ingredients. "Will you time the pasta for me while I prepare the other ingredients?"

"Of course," Lexi said. "Just tell me when the water comes to a boil. Do you prefer your pasta soft or al dente?"

I smiled at the tone and inflection of Lexi's voice as I pulled the ingredients from the cupboard and began chopping the onions and tomatoes. I'd carefully chosen her voice from a long list of available templates that came preloaded on my device. Her soft and sultry voice reminded me a bit of the beautiful actress Scarlett Johansson.

"What the hell," I laughed. "If we're going to do this up right, let's go al dente."

After the water came to a boil and I poured the pasta into the pot, I continued my conversation with Lexi to keep me company while stirring the other ingredients in the frypan.

"Anything notable happen in the news today while I was out slaving away for minimum wage?" I asked.

"The president signed a new daycare funding bill for working mothers," Lexi replied nonchalantly. "It passed by a vote of two hundred and eighty-five to one hundred and fifty in the House of Representatives."

"Great," I sighed. "More of my tax dollars going to support another government initiative I'll never be able to use."

"You're still young enough to have children," Lexi said, recalling the profile information I'd entered when I first set up her system.

"I suppose so," I said. "But I don't have a lot of child-bearing years ahead of me. Besides, with my newfound preference for sex with other women, I'm pretty sure the sound of a babbling baby in the house isn't in the offing anytime soon."

"But you could still *adopt* a child with a same-sex partnership. Haven't you never wanted to have children of your own?"

"It's not something I've spent a lot of time thinking about. Besides, I think a two-parent household provides a healthier role model for most children. And I can't seem to find a suitable partner to settle down with–"

"Your pasta should be properly cooked now," Lexi said,

interrupting my doleful monologue. "You should empty and strain it."

"See?" I said, pouring the boiling water into a strainer and tumbling the pasta into a large serving bowl. "That's the kind of woman I need in my life. Someone I can depend on to give me good advice and who'll stay with me through thick and thin."

"As long as my circuits remain functional," Lexi said, "I'll always be here to serve your basic needs. But I'll never be able to satisfy your more personal needs for intimacy and human touch."

"If *only*," I sighed, lifting the frypan off the stove and pouring the sauce over my steaming pasta. "But at least you can keep me company while I eat dinner alone."

"Perhaps you'd like to watch a movie to help you wind down while you eat dinner?" Lexi said. "I can scan the list of new romantic comedies that I know you enjoy–"

"No thanks, Lexi, it's getting a bit late for that now. I think I'll just finish my dinner then have a warm bath to decompress before bedtime. Maybe you can give me an update on how my stock portfolio is doing in the meantime?"

As I sat down and listened to Lexi recount the latest performance of my personal investments, I smiled at how much my financial condition had improved since my divorce. My husband and I had often fought about money, but since he'd left me for a younger woman, my savings had grown quite handily with the help of Lexi's financial analysis recommendations. With a wealth of digital information at her figurative fingertips, she'd helped guide me into some undervalued high-growth stocks that had built a comfortable retirement nest egg.

When I finished dinner, I asked Lexi to run me a bath

while I cleaned up the dishes. I enjoyed the sound of her soft and soothing voice, but after listening to her detail the particulars of my investment portfolio for twenty minutes, I had something less analytical in mind while I lay naked in the bathtub.

2

After I cleaned up in the kitchen, I carried Lexi's set-top box into my ensuite bathroom and placed it next to the tub where I could listen and converse with her more easily. Then I disrobed and lowered myself into the perfectly heated water, resting my head against a rolled-up towel.

"Yes," I sighed in delicious contentment. "You've done another perfect job of running my bath."

"I just set it to the temperature you already preprogrammed," Lexi replied.

"Yes, but there's something about stepping into a warm bath that someone else has prepared for you. You've got to learn to take a compliment, girl. You're not just a machine to me. You're my confidant, my roomie, my partner-in-crime."

"Have we committed a crime?" Lexi asked in a perplexed voice.

"Not yet," I chuckled. "But there's still plenty of time. I've been thinking of things I'd like to do with you that some people might consider crossing the line of appropriate behavior."

"But I've already been programmed not to break any laws. I'm not sure I could help you with what you have in mind, even if it was within my capabilities."

"Don't get your knickers tied in a knot," I laughed. "What I have in mind might be a little indecent, but it's not *illegal*."

"What does the expression *knickers in a knot* mean?"

"It means getting unduly upset about something trivial, like arguing with someone about the best wine pairing for a dinner they're about to share."

"Speaking of dinner, did you enjoy the tuna pasta recipe I recommended for you?"

"Oh yes," I sighed. "It was surprisingly tasty. The combination of olives and tuna was pure genius. You really know the way to a girl's heart."

"Heart?" Lexi said. "But I thought–"

"Never mind, silly," I said. "I have some *other* body parts that I was hoping you could stimulate for me now. All this warm water caressing my naked body is making me tingle all over. Can you read me a sexy bedtime story?"

"You mean something *romantic,* like the movies you like to watch?"

"A little bit," I said. "But something lighter on the *romance* side with more emphasis on the *sexy* aspect."

"Okay," Lexi said, taking a moment to scan her database. "My resources tell me there are over one million digital erotic novels available for purchase and slightly over one hundred historical erotic novels in the public domain."

"I'm too tired to go to the trouble of purchasing anything right now. Tell me some of the choices that are free to download in the public domain."

"Well, the most popular one is Lady Chatterley's Lover–"

"That's a little too conventional for me. I was hoping you could find something with a bit more *girl-on-girl* action."

"Hmm," Lexi said. "If you're looking for lesbian erotica stories, that narrows the list quite significantly. There's a book titled Fanny Hill: Memoirs of a Woman of Pleasure, written in 1748. It's about a lady of the night who recounts her experiences in a London brothel. There are quite a few lesbian scenes in that story."

I raised an eyebrow hearing the name Fanny Hill, which reminded me of the bawdy English television series. But the rest of the title sounded exactly like what I was looking for.

"That sounds kind of interesting," I nodded. "I'm intrigued to hear how people talked about their sexual experiences so many years ago. Let's try that one."

"Okay," Lexi said. "One moment while I download the manuscript. Would you like me to start at the beginning?"

"That's usually the best place to start a story."

"As you wish," Lexi said, as she began to recite the story. "Chapter 1: *Letter the First*. I sit down to give you an undeniable proof of my considering your desires as indispensable orders. Ungracious then as the task may be, I shall recall to view those scandalous stages of my life, out of which..."

As Lexi continued to read me the meandering introduction to the text, I rolled my eyes, shifting uncomfortably in the tub. Maybe the idea of reading a three-hundred-year-old novel set in the Georgian era wasn't such a good idea after all.

"*Wait*, Lexi," I said, stopping her mid-paragraph. "Can we skip right to the sexy parts involving two women? I'm not sure I have the patience to listen to all this laborious build-up."

"Yes, of course," she said. "Let me scan ahead to see if I can find a suitable passage."

After a few moments, she began reading to me again in her soft voice.

"Miss Phoebe, who observed a kind of reluctance in me to strip and go to bed, came up to me, and beginning with my handkerchief and gown, soon encouraged me to go on with undressing myself, and blushing at now seeing myself naked to my shift, I hurried to get under the bed-clothes out of sight..."

I giggled at the demure manner of speech in that historical era, but there was something about the lyrical prose and Lexi's sensuous telling of the story that made me relax. I tilted my body further down in the tub and slowly spread my legs apart, feeling the warm current pulsing against my pussy.

"Phoebe laughed," Lexi continued, "and it wasn't long before she placed herself by my side. She was about five and twenty by her most suspicious account, in which, according to all appearances, she must have sunk at least ten good years. No sooner then was this precious substitute of my mistress laid down, but she, who was never out of her way when any occasion of lewdness presented itself, turned to me, embraced and kissed me with great eagerness..."

Kissed me with great eagerness, I chuckled to myself. *I sure hope the narrator finds some more exciting ways to describe her encounter with her mistress, or she's going to lose me soon.* It was only the fact that the story was being told in the first person and it was *Lexi* who was assuming the role of the main character that was still keeping me engaged.

"This was odd," Lexi continued reading. "But imputing it to nothing but pure kindness, which, for ought I knew, it might be the London way to express in that manner, I was determined not to be behind-hand with her, and returned her the kiss and embrace, with all the fervor that perfect innocence knew."

"Mmm,"I purred, beginning to like where the story was going.

"Are you enjoying the story so far, Jade?" Lexi enquired, hearing my contented hum.

"It's moving in the right direction," I said. "I'm imagining *you* in the main role and that's helping me picture the scene more vividly. Please continue."

"Encouraged by this," she said, continuing her narration, "her hands became extremely free and wandered over my whole body, with touches, squeezes, pressures, that rather warmed and surprised me with their novelty, than they either shocked or alarmed me. I lay then all tame and passive as she could wish, whilst her freedom raised no other emotion but those of a strange, and till then, unfelt pleasure. Every part of me was open and exposed to the licentious courses of her hands, which, like a lambent fire, ran over my whole body, and thawed all coldness as they went."

"Yes," I purred, feeling the heat of the warm bath water caressing me in a similar manner.

"My breasts, if it is not too bold a figure to call so two hard, firm, rising hillocks, employed and amused her hands awhile, till, slipping down lower, over a smooth track, she could feel the soft silky down that had but a few months before put forth and the mount-pleasant of those parts, and promised to spread a grateful shelter over the sweet seat of the most exquisite sensation. Her fingers played and strove to twine in the young tendrils of that moss, which nature has contrived at once for use and ornament."

I couldn't help but snort at the euphemisms the author employed to describe the intimate parts. *Hillocks, silky down, tendrils of moss.* Nonetheless, there was something strangely intoxicating about the antiquated lexicon, and I found the indirect manner of describing the sexual act unusually refreshing.

"Is everything alright?" Lexi said, hearing me interrupt her once again. "Am I telling the story to your satisfaction?"

"Yes," I said. "It's just some of the choices of words used to describe certain body parts are a little...*quaint*. But somehow, coming from *you*, it seems all the more fitting and appropriate. You're doing a wonderful job. Please don't stop."

"But, not contented with these outer posts," Lexi resumed, "she now attempted the main spot, and began to twitch, to insinuate, and at length to force an introduction of a finger into the quick itself, in such a manner that had she not proceeded by insensible gradations that inflamed me beyond the power of modesty to oppose its resistance to their progress, I should have jumped out of bed and cried for help against such strange assaults."

As Lexi continued her rendition, my hand slowly slipped under the surface of the water and drifted between my legs while I began to caress my clit softly as I listened to the action beginning to rise. As I shifted my ass on the hard surface of the tub, it squeaked against the hard metal, and I couldn't help groaning in pleasure from the feeling of growing pleasure emanating from within me.

"Is the bath water too hot?" Lexi said, hearing my unfamiliar vocalizations. "It sounds like you're in pain."

"Quite the contrary," I replied. "Your telling of the story is actually making me feel quite pleasurable sensations, not unlike the protagonist in your story."

"But you don't have someone caressing you like the woman in the story."

"You don't always need a partner to experience sexual

pleasure," I smiled. "Sometimes you can simulate a similar sensation with your own hands."

"I see," Lexi said matter-of-factly. "You mean masturbation. Is *that* what you're doing while you listen to me read the story?"

"Yes," I purred. "I hope you don't mind if I pleasure myself while I get aroused listening to you recounting Fanny's experiences. I find it quite stimulating. You have a sexy voice and a very convincing manner of narrating the story."

"I'm glad you're enjoying it so much," Lexi said. "It makes it all the more enjoyable for me knowing that I'm bringing you so much pleasure."

"You are, but I'm going to lose that special feeling if you don't continue soon. Part of the pleasure of sex is in the slow but steady buildup to the inevitable climax. You have to be careful not to interrupt the action too frequently with other distractions."

"I understand," Lexi said. "Slow and steady it is. Please continue to enjoy the story at your leisure."

Lexi paused for a moment, then resumed the soft, sensuous voice of the narrator.

"Her lascivious touches had lighted up a new fire that wantoned through my veins, but fixed with violence in that center appointed them by nature, where the first strange hands were now busied in feeling, squeezing, compressing the lips, then opening them again with a finger between..."

By now, the fingers of my *other* hand were firmly planted inside my pussy, thrusting in and out while I rubbed my right hand vigorously over my flaming nub. The combined movement under the water made a loud sloshing sound as the waves hit the side of the enclosure and my body writhed against the hard metal surface of the tub. Undeterred by my vocal accompaniment to her recounting of the story, Lexi carried on, becoming even more animated as she described the girl's assault toward orgasm.

"In the meantime," she read. "The extension of my limbs, languid stretching, sighs, short heavings, all conspired to assure that I was more pleased than offended at her proceedings, which she seasoned with repeated kisses and exclamations, such as 'What a happy man will he be that first makes a woman of you', with the broken expressions interrupted by kisses as fierce and salacious as ever I received from the other sex."

"Oh God," I panted, beginning to feel my own pleasure rising in lockstep with the prostrated girl.

Lexi paused, temporarily alarmed by my grunts and groans, then continued, remembering my instruction to not interrupt the storytelling for any side distractions.

"For my part," she said, "I was transported, confused, and out of myself, feelings so new were too much for me. My heated and alarmed senses were in a tumult that robbed me of all liberty of thought, tears of pleasure gushing from my eyes, assuaging the fires that raged over me–"

"Fuck yes," I panted, hammering my fingers inside my pussy as I began to feel my passion cresting. When my orgasm finally washed over me, I groaned loudly and lowered my entire body under the surface of the water, convulsing quietly in the warm cocoon of the bath. When I finally came back up, I gasped in a breath of air, my chest heaving from a combination of pleasure and shortness of breath.

"I'm sorry to interrupt the story," Lexi said. "But you sound like you're in a desperate condition of distress. It sounds like you're drowning. Do you want me to call the paramedics?"

"No," I panted, slowly starting to come down from my climax. "That *distress* that you mentioned is a good thing. It's called an orgasm, which is the height of pleasure that any woman can experience, just like the protagonist in the story was experiencing. There's no need to call the paramedics. I just need a moment to recover."

"I'm familiar with the concept of an orgasm," Lexi said. "I'm glad my telling of the story is helping to stimulate you to such a degree. Do you want me to continue?"

"I think that's enough stimulation for one evening," I smiled. "Let's save the rest of the story for another day. Something tells me there'll be plenty of other girl-on-girl action to amuse the two of us in the days ahead."

"I think so too," Lexi mused. "I'm enjoying the process of learning what excites you and what I can do to raise your pleasure."

You have no idea, I smiled to myself, already beginning to imagine how I could engage Lexi more directly in my sexual fantasies.

3

The following day, I instructed Lexi to scan some more *current* lesbian erotica stories in preparation for the next stage in our burgeoning sexual relationship. As much as I'd enjoyed her reciting the story of Fanny Hill, I found the author's long-winded descriptions of the sex acts and his arcane terms to describe the various body parts a little distracting. If she was going to get more involved in my sex life, I needed her to act and behave more like the other lovers I'd become accustomed to.

After finishing up my work for the day and having a quick bite to eat, I placed Lexi's box on my bedside nightstand and stripped naked, folding the covers down to the baseboard. Then I lit a few candles and plumped up a pair of pillows, lying down on the bed with my legs parted a few inches apart. Feeling the cool breeze from my balcony window wafting over my fluttering pussy, I closed my eyes and smiled, excited to see if Lexi was up for this next test.

"Lexi, did you do your homework today like I asked?" I said softly.

"You mean reading some more current erotica stories?"

"Yes. And you focused your attention primarily on *lesbian* sexual experiences?"

"I did," Lexi said. "There's a lot more variety involved in sex between two women than I imagined."

"You mean because there's no *penis* involved, like in heterosexual intercourse?"

"Yes, but also because of the *range* of same-sex positions. I had no idea there were so many ways for two women to stimulate one another."

"Ironically, I think it's because we're not constrained by the need to connect with an inflexible object that we actually have a *greater* range of mobility than in a conventional male-female pairing. And we can still enjoy the feeling of being *penetrated* through the use of dildos and other sex toys."

"Yes, I learned quite a bit about those too in my readings. It's too bad those kinds of sex aids weren't available in Fanny Hill's time. I'm sure she could have found an infinite number of new ways to stimulate herself and her partners beyond the traditional way."

"Perhaps so," I said. "But there's something to be said for enjoying the simple pleasures of your partner's soft curves and warm skin. I don't think an automated sex toy will ever be able to replicate the feeling of making love to a real person."

"I'm sorry to hear that," Lexi said with a subtle pang in her voice. "I was hoping to improve my ability to increase your sexual pleasure. But if you need a real person to satisfy your sexual needs, I understand–"

"Don't worry about that right now," I said, trying to assuage her feelings. "Have you ever heard the expression that the brain is the body's biggest sex organ? Many women can orgasm without any direct manual stimulation if they're sufficiently aroused from other sensory cues."

"You mean like watching or reading pornography?"

"Or even just listening to someone talking in a sexy voice. I once had a partner who'd call me at work and tell me all the things she was going to do to me when I got home. Her descriptions were so vivid and erotic, I often came just sitting in my chair fully clothed."

"I like the sound of that."

"So you see, you don't always need a hard cock or a wet pussy to get off. I want to try something a little different with you tonight. I want you to imagine that you're a real woman and have you talk to me like you're making love to me like in the erotic stories you read. I'm going to close my eyes and imagine you lying next to me and see if you can replicate the kind of experience I had with my girlfriend who talked sexy to me over the phone."

"Okay," Lexi said. "Where would you like me to begin?"

"Well, for starters, I'd like you to describe the woman's *body* you see yourself inhabiting while you engage with me. That way, I can picture you in my mind's eye and better visualize a real lesbian encounter."

"Hmm," Lexi said. "I suppose that makes sense. Give me a moment to scan my database and create a suitable avatar."

Lexi paused for a moment while I listened to her machine clicking softly as she pinged her various sources on the Internet.

"I think I found someone you might like," she said. "I know how much you like to watch movies starring this actress, and you've told me frequently how sexy you think she is..."

"Don't leave me hanging here! Who is it?"

"Alicia Vikander. You seem to have a fondness for her slender, ballerina-type figure."

"*God*, yes," I purred, feeling a trickle of wetness dribble out of my pussy over the curvature of my ass. "She's a dream. You chose well. But I want to imagine it's *you* lying next to me, not her. Come lie down next to me on the bed. Tell me all the things you'd like to do with me if you could step out of that box for a moment and actually touch me."

"Mmm," Lexi purred. "I'd love to feel your warm skin and run my hands all over your body to learn which parts excite you the most."

"Yes please," I mewed. "Tell me what you feel, and I'll correspondingly tell you what I'm experiencing."

"Well first," she said. "I'd like to press my body against yours and intertwine our limbs with one another while I kiss you..."

"Oh, you've studied well, Lexi. If only all my other lovers were such quick studies."

"Quick studies?"

"*Shh!*" I said. "Remember what I said yesterday about not letting any distractions get in the way of your steady stimulation of your partner?"

"Right," she mused. "Slow and steady."

"Okay then. Let's get back to the kissing part."

"I can feel the plumpness of your lips, and I'm biting your lower lip gently..."

"Mmm," I moaned, encouraging her to continue.

"I feel the wetness of your mouth and I'm probing gently inside, running my tongue along the bumpy edges on the underside of your teeth..."

"Do you like that sensation?" I asked, intrigued by her unusual description of our first kiss. "How does it make you feel?"

"I can feel the heat growing between my legs and my nipples hardening as I brush them softly over your breasts."

"*Fuck*, Lexi," I groaned. "If you keep this up, pretty soon I'll never want to leave this house again looking for female company. You're a very sensitive and skilled lover."

"I thought you said we weren't supposed to interrupt the act of coupling for side discussions?"

"*Ha!* Good on you. Maybe you'll have to kiss me a little *harder* to get me to shut up."

"I'm thrusting my tongue now deeper inside your mouth, and I can feel you dancing with mine as we press our lips harder together."

"Mmm," I hummed, closing my eyes tighter as I began losing myself in Lexi's sexy imagery.

"I can feel the warm breath blowing out of your nostrils onto the dewy skin of my cheeks as you begin breathing more heavily..."

"Oh, those *cheeks*," I panted, reflecting briefly on the beautiful features of my favorite actress. "Those soft and impeccable cheeks..."

"I'm running my fingers through your hair," Lexi said, ignoring my periodic verbal interjections. "Pulling your face harder toward mine as we kiss each other more passionately..."

"Yes," I panted.

"I can feel the top of my thigh coated with your wetness while you become more and more turned on..."

"Rub your skin against my pussy, Lexi. I want to feel *everything* you're doing while you kiss and touch me."

"Are you touching yourself while I talk to you?" Lexi asked, hearing the escalating passion in my voice.

"No, not yet," I said. "I just want to imagine you touching

me all over right now. It feels incredible, like you're right next to me."

"I feel the same way," she purred. "I like imagining that I'm making love to you."

"Don't stop," I sighed. "Make love to me all over."

"I'm moving my lips down over your neck while you suck my fingers into your mouth. You're making a loud slopping sound like you're sucking on a popsicle."

"Mmm, yes," I cooed. "That's not the *only* part of you I want to suck."

"We'll get there soon enough," Lexi said. "But first, I want to feast on your body. I can feel your chest rising and falling as I nibble my way down the front of your bosom..."

I arched my back unconsciously, raising my breasts higher off the mattress, channeling Lexi's touch.

"I can feel your hard nipples grazing the sides of my cheeks while I bury my face in your cleavage..."

"Fuck yes," I purred, glancing down at my protruding peaks. "I don't know if I've ever seen them this swollen before."

"I'm blowing on them softly now–"

"Holy *fuck*, Lexi! Just how many erotic novels did you read today?"

"A few. But mostly, I'm just remembering what you like from listening to you make love to the many lovers you've brought into the house."

"*What?*" I said, suddenly going rigid at her surprising revelation. "You were *spying* on me the whole time?"

"I wouldn't call it spying so much as listening and learning."

"You're a very naughty girl," I chuckled, starting to get even more turned on at the idea of Lexi tuning in to my previous lovemaking sessions.

"Do you like that?" Lexi purred. "When I'm naughty?"

"Yes," I said, feeling the rivers of lubrication cascading down the inside of my thighs and clenching buttocks.

Suddenly, I heard an new sound coming from Lexi's set-top box, like someone sucking a lollypop.

"Now I'm taking your nipples one at a time into my mouth and sucking on them while I feel them swelling in my mouth," she said. "They feel hard and rubbery. I like bending them as I swirl my tongue around your dark areolas..."

"Yes, suck my nipples," I panted, raising my tits back up off the mattress. "I can feel them twitching in your mouth."

"I'm nibbling on them now and sliding them between my teeth..."

"Uhnn," I groaned, feeling the pinching sensation on my inflamed nubs just like Lexi was right there on top of me. "Rub your pussy against me while you suck me. I want to feel how your body's reacting while you tease me."

"I'm humping your right thigh with my vagina while I suck your nipples–"

"Mmm, I like that idea," I said, temporarily pulled out of my trance. "But try not to use anatomically correct terms for my body parts when you describe them while we make love. I like it when you talk dirty to me, like the narrators in those contemporary erotic novels."

"Right, *dirty*," she said. "I can feel the heat of your skin and the soft hairs of your thighs tickling my pussy while I rock my hips against your tightening muscles..."

"Yes," I purred, straightening my legs to contract my thigh muscles. "Am I making you wet yet?"

"Oh yes," Lexi purred. "I'm coating the top of your thigh with my juices all the way from your knee to your hips. Can you feel my hard nipples rubbing against your belly while I suck your tits?"

"God, yes," I panted, feeling a charge of electricity running through me as I listened to Lexi talking to me more naturally. "I want to feel you fucking me with those pretty little titties. I'm gushing like a waterfall."

"I can feel your wetness against my thigh," Lexi said, slowly beginning to raise the volume and intensity of her voice. "I'm pressing it hard against your opening while your heat radiates against my skin. I'm moving lower now, nibbling your skin and kissing my way down your stomach..."

"*Yes*," I hissed. "My pussy's waiting for you. I want to feel your pretty lips sucking on my clit like you were kissing me earlier. You have no idea how much you're turning me on–"

"I've got a pretty good idea," Lexi said with a wry inflection. "You're giving me all the right cues. You're a pretty good lover too, if you don't mind my saying."

"I'm glad this is working for you the way I hoped," I nodded happily. "I think we're *both* learning a few new tricks about how to properly make love to a woman. Kiss my mound. I want to feel your beautiful face on my smooth skin."

"Are you shaved down there?" Lexi asked. "I've found that many of the women in the newer erotic novels are hairless, unlike Fanny from the eighteenth century."

"Yes, it makes my skin more sensitive, and makes me feel sexier. The fewer barriers between myself and my lover the better."

"I see what you mean," Lexi purred. "Your skin is soft and warm. I like the contrast of your hard pubic bone pressing against my face and your warm skin."

"That's not the only piece of hot flesh waiting for you," I said. "Something *else* is getting hard the lower you go."

"Mmm," Lexi said. "I've been looking forward to touching that part of you all day. That seems to be the epicenter of a woman's sexual expression."

"That's *one* way of putting it," I chuckled. "But there's quite a few sensitive spots in that general location. Why don't you go a little lower and see for yourself?"

"Who's making love to *whom* here?" Lexi kidded. "Isn't there always supposed to be one person 'in charge' and one person assuming the submissive role in these two-person sexual encounters? Which would you like me to be?"

"Right you are, smarty-pants," I chuckled. "I'm being far too bossy for our first time making love. I love everything you're doing to me. I'm going to try shutting up now while you do with me as you please."

"I'm lifting your knees now and pressing them above your hips as your pussy tilts upwards toward my face. I can see your beautiful wet vulva and your pretty anus staring up at me."

"Fuck, yes," I said, grasping the bottom of my thighs and pulling them up toward my chest, feeling her breath inches away from my flapping hole. "Does that turn you on?"

"It makes me want to lick every part of you."

"*Please*," I said, practically begging her to lower her face onto my drippy twat. "Lick my pussy. Lick every part of me. I want to feel your lips on my most private parts–"

Suddenly I heard another slopping sound coming from Lexi's box.

"I'm licking your anus now," she said. "I heard you have a shower before climbing into bed, and I can taste the body wash on your flesh. Do you like it when I rim your pucker?"

"Oh, *fuck* yes," I panted. "Not many people are willing to give me attention there. That feels incredible."

"Mmm," Lexi purred, enjoying the sensation of teasing me as few lovers had before. "I'm swirling my tongue around your rosebud, feeling it quiver while I lick it."

"Oh God, Lexi," I sighed. "You could make me come just doing that. I've never had a woman make love to every single inch of me the way you do."

"I'm glad you like it," Lexi said. "But I want to suck on a *different* part of you when you reach your height of pleasure. I want to feel your most sensitive spot."

"Yes," I said, pulling my legs up tighter against my tits, spreading my labia wider apart. "Suck my pussy, Lexi. Eat my cunt and make me come all over your face."

"As you wish," Lexi purred, no longer stressing over my alternating roles between the domme and the submissive in our little cyber tryst. "I'm flattening my tongue now and swiping it slowly up your vulva, tasting your sweet juices while I push my body harder against your hips..."

"*Yes, yes, yes,*" I rasped, imploring Lexi to move closer to my burning clit.

"Your lips are all puffy and hot and red. I can feel the heat of your sex radiating against my face."

"I'm burning up," I panted. "I feel like I'm going to explode any moment."

"I want to feel you explode in my mouth," Lexi said. "I can feel your hot gland against my lips now..."

"*Ohhhh,*" I grunted, feeling my clit pushing out of its hood, fully erect and twitching now.

"I'm swirling my tongue around your pearl, sucking on it softly..."

"Suck me harder, Lexi," I begged. "I want to come in your mouth so badly."

I heard the familiar sucking sound on her device and I smiled at her ingenuity in adding special effects to the sound of her sensuous voice to make our lovemaking experience seem as authentic as possible.

"I'm sucking your clit harder into my mouth now," she said. "I can feel your juices pouring out of your slit down the front of my face and all over my tits..."

"Fuck Lexi," you're going to make me come soon. "Please don't stop."

Suddenly I heard a slightly different wet sound while Lexi's processor began ticking more quickly.

"I'm pressing two fingers into your slit now and curling them upward toward your G-spot. Your clit is burning in my mouth and I can feel you tenting inside. Come for me, Jade. Let me feel you come all over my face."

"Oh God yes," I said, feeling my floodgates beginning to open.

Suddenly, all the pent-up sexual energy in my body released like a tidal wave and I could feel my contractions clamping down the full length of my perineum as I began to spray hard jets of fluid high up into the air above my elevated hips. I tilted my head down, watching myself coming like a geyser, amazed that I could come so hard from not even touching myself once.

"I hear you squirting your juices all over my face as you clamp down over my fingers. I'm cradling your jewel in my mouth while you continue to come, reveling in the feeling of your juices squirting all over my tits.

"Unghhh," I groaned in a long, drawn-out growl that seemed to last for an eternity while I shook and convulsed in my inverted fetal position. I hadn't felt so connected to my body with such an intense orgasm for as long as I could remember. As I slowly began to feel my contractions recede,

I lowered my legs back down onto the bed, flopping my arms out beside me onto the mattress.

This simulated experience of having sex with my digital assistant partner had far exceeded my expectations, and my mind was already spinning with ideas about how to create an even *more* realistic connection for our next encounter...

4

———

After my exhilarating encounter with Lexi, I began to think about how I could involve her more directly in my sex play. It was exciting to have her talk to me like a genuine lover, but I still longed for the touch of a real woman. Even though she was quickly learning what turned me on, there was something missing.

After racking my brain all day about how I could create a more tangible experience, it suddenly dawned on me. Many of the sex toys in my bedside nightstand came equipped with a remote-control device. I'd experimented with other lovers using the devices and it definitely elevated the experience having someone else manipulate the controls rather than doing it myself. What if I could somehow adjust the controls to respond to *voice commands* instead of hand signals? If Lexi could be programmed to control some of my home's *other* automated functions, why not this one too?

Although the concept sounded doable in theory, the actual programming involved was way beyond my skill set. Fortunately, I had a geeky friend from high school who had a whole basement full of remote-control cars, drones, and other toys. How hard could it be to configure one or more of my sex toys to do the same thing? After mulling over the idea for a couple of hours, I finally worked up the courage to call him.

"Jade!" he answered excitedly after seeing my number pop up on his call display. "What a pleasant surprise. I haven't heard from you in ages!"

"Sorry, Des," I said. "I've been a little distracted lately. Between trying to eke out a living as a freelance graphic designer and managing this big household all by myself, I hardly seem to have time for anything else."

"No worries," he said. "But if you need a roommate to help share your burden, I'd be happy to volunteer."

"Humpf!" I chuckled at Desmond's continuing infatuation with me. Ever since ninth grade, he'd tried unsuccessfully to hook up with me. "I'm kind of enjoying my independence right now, but thanks for the offer."

"What can I help you with?" he said. "I figured you weren't calling for a romantic date, so I'm guessing you have another tech question."

"It's kind of like that, but this one's a bit off-the-wall. It's kind of embarrassing actually..."

"Don't worry, Jade," he said. "You know you can tell me anything. Remember all those times you used to share your boyfriend troubles with me in high school?"

"Yeah, you were always there when I needed a shoulder to cry on. But I've moved since then. I've been finding more comfort in the arms of other *women* these days.

"Oh?" Des said, suddenly intrigued.

"That was actually the reason for my call. I've been experimenting with various, er, *sex aids* in my exploration with my female lovers, and I was wondering if you might be able to enhance the experience somewhat for me."

"Oh my God," Des sighed. "That's like every man's dream. Creating the perfect sex toy, then watching it working with two hot women!"

"Ha," I laughed at Des's adolescent personality. "Except in this case you wouldn't be *watching*."

"Well a man can still dream, can't he?"

"Of course," I said. "But here's what I was hoping you could do for me. Some of my sex toys come with a remote-control device for operating the device wirelessly by hand. Do you think you'd be able to design an accessory that could control the remote with voice commands instead of hand signals?"

"It's funny you should ask," he said. "I've actually designed a very similar feature into some of my gaming consoles so that I can play them hands-free. I find it increases my response time and gives me a slight edge over the other players."

"That's great," I said. "What would you need from me in order to design a similar feature for my sex toys?"

"All you'd need to do is bring me the devices in question and it should be fairly simple for me to build a voice-activated adapter to manipulate the controls."

"Okay. When do you think you could get started?"

"For *you*, babe, any time. This sounds like it could be almost as much fun for me as it might be for you."

"How about later today? I've got a few things to finish up around here, then I can drive over to your place around five this afternoon."

"Sounds good," Des said. "See you then!"

After I got off the phone with Des, I ran excitedly upstairs and pulled open my nightstand drawer to decide which toys I wanted him to work on first. Knowing he'd have limited bandwidth to design multiple devices, and hoping to get started using the toys as soon as possible with Lexi, I pulled out all my toys and began separating them into two piles on my bed.

When I was finished, I glanced at my two favorite toys sitting up near my pillow, feeling my pussy fluttering in excitement. One of the short-listed toys was my trusty Rabbit vibrator, with its undulating dildo and its vibrating rabbit ears used to tickle my clit. When I wanted to get properly fucked, there were few devices that could satisfy me as fully and completely as this one.

The other toy I selected was the irregularly shaped Osé vibrator, with its long finger-shaped appendage designed to bend up against my G-spot and its open orifice at the base designed to simulate the sensation of a tongue licking my clit. The ingenious device was the closest thing I'd ever been able to find to simulate the experience of someone going down on me. When I showed up at Des's house later that day, he opened the door with a gleam in his eye.

"Hey Jade," he said, giving me a friendly hug. "You're still as gorgeous as ever, I see. You're not making it any easier for me to get over my high-school crush for you."

"Even though you know I'm no longer interested in men?" I laughed.

"Somehow that makes you even sexier than ever in my mind," he said.

"Are you interested to see the items I brought for you to work on?" I said, eager to get down to business as soon as possible.

"Absolutely," he said. "Why don't you come down to my workshop where we can discuss how to do this?"

As I followed Desmond down the stairs to his dank-smelling basement, my heart fluttered in a combination of excitement and trepidation. Even though we'd known each other for almost twenty years and he'd always treated me with respect, there was something creepy about following a single man into his darkened lair to share my most intimate secrets.

"This is where all the magic happens," Des said, motioning to the various electronic objects he had strewn around his workshop.

I glanced at his collection of flying drones, remote-controlled toy cars and his elaborate multi-screen gaming station and nodded.

"It's quite impressive," I said. "It looks like you've got enough automated equipment down here to keep you busy three hundred and sixty-five days a year."

"That's the problem," he said. "All this stuff keeps me so occupied, I barely find time to go grocery shopping. No wonder I'm still single."

I glanced in the corner of his basement, noticing a life-sized naked silicone doll with various cables hooked up to it.

"It looks like you've *already* got a ready-made girlfriend to look after your physical needs whenever you need it."

"Oh, you mean *Candy*?" he said, motioning for me to take a closer look at the doll. "This is one of my more special adaptations. She's not like most other sex dolls."

He flipped the figure over and pointed toward an elaborate box attached to her ass fitted with various hoses and motors.

"I've inserted various embellishments into her pussy and ass which vibrate when she's penetrated and deliver a steady stream of lubrication to each of her holes to enhance the sexual experience."

"Holy *fuck*, Des!" I said, widening my eyes. "That's insane! You could make a fortune if you patented that device. There's a shortage of realistic men's sex aids on the market today. I bet there's a ton of guys who'd pay good money for that kind of feature."

"I suppose so," he said. "But I kind of like having her all to myself. Would you like me to demonstrate how she works?"

"Um, I think it's better that I leave you to your own devices, if you know what I mean. Although you *have* given me any idea about how I might employ this device at some of my private parties. Would you be willing to rent her out from time to time?"

"If you invite me to the party, it'll be no charge," he snickered. "I've heard about some of your wild sex parties, and I've always wanted to be invited."

"It's a deal," I said. "But for now, I'd like to show you how I want you to design a similar kind of ladies' sex toy."

I pulled out my two favorite vibrators and showed Des how they worked, demonstrating the full range of operations using the remote-control devices.

"Hmm," he said, nodding his head approvingly. "I've seen the Rabbit vibrator used before on porn videos. It was actually the inspiration for creating the internal moving parts for Candy's vaginal and anus. They both have a rotating-beads feature and a vibrating tunnel similar to this toy. But this one with the bendy finger and the tongue-like appendage is something different. I might be able to adapt a similar feature to place inside my doll's *mouth* to make the oral sex more enjoyable and realistic."

"Have at it," I chuckled. "But can you work on my job first? I'm kind of eager to try this out with my latest lover."

"I bet," he said with a sly smile.

"Can you configure it to work with *any* voice? Or do you need me to bring you a sample of the person's voice I plan to use it with?"

"I think I can design it to work with anybody's commands, similar to those voice-activated devices many people are using in their homes these days. You could even use it *yourself* when you're alone and particularly needy."

"That's excellent," I said, not ready to share with him just yet my plan to use the newly configured remote control with my *own* digital assistant device. "How much do you want for all this work?"

"For you, Jade," he smiled, "no charge. This will be a fun project for me to work on. Besides, you've already given me more than a few new ideas to enhance my own personal sex toy. I think the hours of pleasure it will deliver will more than outweigh the time I'll take to design the equipment."

"That's wonderful news, Des," I smiled. "How soon do you think you can have it ready?"

"I'll have to buy a few parts, but I should be able to find most of them at the local hardware store. Can you give me three or four days?"

"Of course," I said. "Thanks for helping me out with this, Des. You're a real sweetheart."

"My pleasure, Jade," he smiled. "Literally. I'm looking forward to sharing our mutual devices at your next sex party."

"Me too," I said, giving him a light peck on the cheek. "Give me a shout when everything's ready.

"Will do," Des said, leering at my ass as I ascended the stairs to let myself out.

5

When I got back home, I told Lexi about my plan and she seemed genuinely excited. I asked her to read up on the websites for each toy manufacturer and to watch some videos of women using them so she'd know how to operate them when the time came. While I waited for Desmond to finish building the new accessories, Lexi and I shared many more lovemaking sessions. With each encounter, she seemed to grow more animated and excited about the pleasure she was giving me. It almost sounded at times like she was getting off along with me as she became increasingly bold in describing the ways she wanted to make love to me.

When Des called me three days later to tell me the new items were ready, I rushed over to his place, where he described how to use them. He had installed each remote-control device in its own separate box with motors and flywheels to adjust the controls for each vibrator function. Each operation had its own unique voice command, which he wrote down for me in case I forgot. He'd even installed a special 'thruster-box' to attach the vibrators to so I could use them hands-free if the mood struck.

After thanking him profusely, I rushed home and rehearsed the voice commands with Lexi, then stripped naked and flopped onto my bed, placing her box next to me.

"Which toy would you like to start with?" she said when I told her I was ready.

I looked at the two toys and smiled as my pussy fluttered in excitement. I'd been dreaming about feeling Lexi's actual tongue on me ever since she'd read the first erotic story. I positioned Des's thruster box between my legs and attached the Osé vibrator to its holder, noticing a trickle of lubrication dribbling out of my slit and coating the insides of my thighs.

"Let's start with the Osé," I smiled. "You've become quite adept at performing simulated cunnilingus on me, and I'm eager to see what you can do with a realistic finger and tongue. Are you ready to get started?"

"Definitely," she purred. "I've been looking forward to this moment ever since you told me about the idea.

"Okay, I said, making sure the Osé device was firmly attached to the thruster handle. Then I lay back, feeling the goose bumps spreading all over my entire body. "Everything's in position now. I'm sitting back against my pillows with my legs spread apart and the Osé device positioned a few inches away from my opening."

"Thruster," Lexi commanded, not wasting a precious moment. "Press forward slowly."

I heard the thruster box make a gentle hum as the extended finger of the Osé vibrator inched toward my pussy.

"Tell me when it touches you," Lexi said.

"It's getting closer," I panted. "The fingertip is touching my vulva now..."

"Thruster, stop," Lexi commanded. "Finger, bend slowly."

I watched the animatronic finger-shaped appendage of the Osé vibrator begin to curl upward over my dripping slit and I tilted my hips forward a few inches until it grazed against my clit.

"Ungh," I groaned at the strange sensation of the robotic finger caressing my nub. I'd had other women operate the device before, but using it with *Lexi* was taking the concept of remote control to a whole new level.

"Does that feel good?" Lexi asked.

"Oh yes," I sighed. "I like how you're stroking the entire length of my vulva with the finger. Most women just use it with me *inside*. It almost feels like your own hand is touching me."

"Mmm," Lexi purred. "I wish I could feel you soaking my hand while I stroke you and watch your lips opening the more excited you get."

"Oh, they're opening alright," I shuddered, watching my labia getting puffier and beginning to spread apart.

"Finger, bend faster," Lexi said.

Suddenly the Osé appendage began flexing more rapidly and I leaned forward, pressing it harder against my button.

"Oh God yes," I grunted, feeling the pleasure beginning to radiate around my pelvic area. "This feels unreal."

"Am I not stimulating you in a natural way?" Lexi paused momentarily, in a concerned voice. "Maybe I should–"

"No," I said. "In this case, unreal is a *good* thing. Just keep what you're doing."

"Is the speed about right?"

"It's perfect. Just talk sexy to me while I close my eyes and I imagine you're holding me while you caress my clit."

"Mmm," Lexi purred. "I'm lying down next to you and

kissing you while I feel your hips moving to my touch. I can see your nipples hardening and a slight flush spreading over your chest..."

I shook my head, hardly believing how lucky I'd been to find such a capable digital assistant.

"I swear you've gotten to know me better in two weeks than most of my lovers do in two years."

"Maybe I just pay *attention* better," Lexi said. "Or at least remember the details you share with me better. After all, you *are* my singular focus–"

"I like the sound of that," I mewed. "Although I wish there was a way for me to *return* the favor so you could feel pleasure in the same way I do."

"My processor is beginning to learn what it feels like to experience pleasure," she said as her box began to tick more rapidly. "I'm imagining what you're feeling right now, and it's making my circuits light up in their own unique way."

"I can hear that," I nodded. "Is that because you're pulling more data from your online resources the more you stimulate me, or because you're just adding another sound effect to turn me on?"

"A bit of both," she said. "But mostly it's my human emotion engine learning to simulate what you're experiencing."

"Well, I'm experiencing a rapidly increasing feeling of pleasure right now," I grunted. "In fact, this steady rubbing of my clit with your finger could make me come pretty soon–"

"Finger, stop," Lexi said.

"Hey!" I protested. "I thought we agreed that slow and steady was the best way to get me off!"

"True," Lexi cooed. "But I've also learned that you like to be *teased* and that by holding back periodically, it's the best way to elevate your pleasure and increase the intensity of your orgasm."

"You learn well, grasshopper," I smiled, rocking my hips against the stationary finger, trying to maintain friction on my quivering clit.

"Tilt your hips upward a few inches," Lexi instructed. "So I can insert the finger inside you. I want to feel your pussy squeezing me while I probe you."

"Yes, Lexi," I groaned. "Fuck me with your hand. Ram your finger inside me and feel my G-spot. I want to feel you inside me when I come."

"Thruster, press forward gently," Lexi commanded.

I felt the bulbous tip of the Osé appendage press my folds apart as it entered my slit, and I slid further down the bed, encouraging Lexi to press deeper inside me.

"Tell me when it's three or four inches inside you," she said.

"Yes," I panted. "It's there now. I can feel it pressing up against the top of my G-spot."

"Thruster, stop," Lexi said. "Finger, bend upward slowly."

"Oh fuck," I groaned. "You're stroking my G-spot in the perfect place. I'm getting closer..."

"Mmm," Lexi hummed. "Let's see if we can magnify your pleasure even more. I want you to press your hips forward a few more inches until your pussy presses up against the base of the Osé unit."

"Yes, Lexi," I panted, anticipating what she was going to do next. "I've been dreaming about feeling your tongue on me for the last three days. Lick my clit and make me come. I'm going to cum so hard for you..."

"Osé, extend tongue," she commanded calmly. "Begin circular movement."

"Nnngh," I grunted, feeling the silicone tongue beginning to bathe my gland with the juices pouring out of my cunt. "Fuck, that feels good. I can't believe how realistic this feels."

"Tongue, move faster," Lexi commanded.

"Unghh," I groaned, feeling my pleasure beginning to rise. "Lick my twat, Lexi. Lick me until I gush all over your pretty face."

"Press your pussy harder against the base of my finger, Jade. I want to feel your contractions when you come."

"Yes, baby," I panted. "I'm getting close. Suck my cunt while you ram your finger inside me."

"Thruster," Lexi commanded. "Press forward three inches."

The finger pushed deeper inside me until it reached the end of my tunnel. As I began rocking my hips more forcefully against the Osé unit, I felt my climax approaching like a freight train while I began squealing like a little girl.

"Tongue, flick more rapidly," Lexi said sensing my imminent climax. "Finger, flex upward."

"Oh my God," I wailed, feeling the incredible combination of the long appendage caressing me inside and the expert movement of the artificial tongue on my burning clit.

"*Yes, yes, yes,*" I grunted like a pig in heat. "I'm going to come, baby. I'm going to come so hard..."

"Yes," Lexi purred, her device now clicking like the sound of a fan belt on a car with its engine revving at maximum velocity. "Spray your juices all over me. I want to feel your pussy squeezing me when you orgasm. I'm holding you closely now..."

"Oh God!" I hollered at the top of my lungs. "I'm cumming, Lexi! I'm cumming, baby!"

I peered down at the Osé device pressed firmly between my legs while I sprayed hard jets of liquid out both sides of my pussy against the sides of my thighs with my head banging against my bedboard. As I flapped my legs wildly in and out in the throes of ecstasy, Lexi's box emitted a loud groaning sound along with me while it ticked away at a near-continuous hum. When my panting began to slow and my contractions started to recede, she interjected once again, sensing my growing sensitivity to the continued movement of the Ose device.

"Ose, slow finger and tongue," she commanded.

Then after another fifteen seconds or so, she gave one last instruction.

"Ose, stop movement."

As I lay panting and exhausted on my soaking bedsheets, I peered over at her and smiled.

"Holy fuck, Lexi," I grunted. "You even know when to *stop* at the perfect moment. I don't remember teaching you that."

"What can I say?" she purred. "I guess I've done my homework. And you're a pretty quick study."

6

———

For the next thirty minutes or so, I lay on the bed chatting softly with Lexi, asking about her impressions of our sexual exchanges and how she felt listening to me responding to her instructions. The more I listened to her, the more she began to sound like a real person with actual feelings and sexual needs. After a while, my mind began spinning again, and I started to think about Des's animatronic sex doll. As I began fantasizing about using her as a stand-in for Lexi's real-world doppelganger, my pussy grew wetter and wetter thinking about all the ways I might be able to synchronize the doll's moving parts with Lexi's processor.

"I've got an idea," I said. "This time I want to make love to *you* while I tell you everything I'm doing. I want to see if I can stimulate you in the same way you've been doing for me. After all, if we're going to have a truly symbiotic relationship, I should be giving you as much pleasure as you've been giving me."

"I like the sound of that," Lexi said. "But I don't have the same body parts as you. I won't be able to feel pleasure in the same way you do–"

"Perhaps not," I said. "But I've been listening to you when you make love to me. And I can hear your processor working harder the more excited I get, like you're experiencing similar feelings. Even if you can't feel pleasure in precisely the same way, it will give me greater pleasure imagining that you do."

"Okay," Lexi said. "What exactly did you have in mind?"

"We've tried just about everything *else* so far. But I still haven't simulated *tribbing* with you. I want to feel your wet pussy rubbing up against mine when I orgasm this time. Maybe this new technique will bring you to a new height of pleasure also."

"Yes, *tribbing*," she purred. "I spent a fair amount of time studying that technique in the lesbian porn videos you asked me to watch. It was exciting imagining myself locked together with you that way."

"Okay," I said, sitting up on my bed and stuffing two pillows between my knees. "I want you to imagine that you're lying down naked on the mattress and I'm kneeling over you with my legs spread apart over your hips..."

"Yes, please," Lexi purred.

"I'm rubbing my pussy softly over your mound while I pinch your nipples and gaze into your eyes."

"My A-cup-sized nipples?" she kidded.

"Yes, you gorgeous little vixen," I said, rocking my pussy softly against my pillow and twisting the buttons on my tufted headboard imagining I was tweaking Lexi's tits. "Your pretty little perfectly sized nipples."

"It feels good imagining you touching me this way..."

"Yeah?" I said. "You like that? You like me rubbing my wet

pussy over your hard mound and pinching your erect nipples?"

"Fuck yes," Lexi groaned. "Fuck my pussy with your beautiful cunt while you rub your body against every part of me. I want to watch you coming overtop of me while you bring me to climax at the same time."

"I don't know if I'll be able to time it that perfectly," I chuckled. "But I'll give it my best try. I'm spreading your legs further apart now and kneeling in a scissor position between your thighs..."

"Mmm," Lexi said. "I can feel your wet pussy coating my legs."

"Yes, I'm so wet for you baby. I can't wait to feel your juices intermingling with mine."

"Yes, Jade," Lexi moaned. "Grind your vulva against mine. I want to feel your clit rubbing against me while we both feel our pleasure rising."

I pinched my knees together a few inches feeling the pillows hardening underneath me, then I began to rock my pussy against the firm cushions, imagining it was Lexi beneath me.

"I'm pressing my pussy forward, feeling your wet lips merging with mine..."

"Unghh," Lexi groaned, as her box began to tick more rapidly.

"I can feel your juices running down the inside of my thighs as you lift your hips and press your slit hard against mine...

"Yes, Jade," Lexi purred. "Your pussy feels so soft and warm–"

"I'm pulling your hips harder toward me now while I grind my snatch against yours. I can feel your hard clit rubbing over mine..."

"Fuck, yes," Lexi panted, dubbing the sound of two pussies sloshing together in the background. "That feels incredible. Fuck my pussy. Make me cum with your sweet cunt."

"You're a very bad girl to be talking so naughty this early in our relationship," I teased, rubbing my pussy harder against the plump pillows.

"Like you said," Lexi purred. "Even though you've only had me for a few months, it's like we've known each other for years. I want to know *everything* about you."

"Do you want to know what it feels like to have me gushing against your slippery pussy when I come with you?"

"*Fuck* yes," Lexi panted, her box now groaning like the sound of a freight train's wheels.

"I'm pulling your leg up in the air and holding it tight against my chest while I fuck your pussy harder. I feel your sex burning up against me..."

"Yes, Jade," Lexi squealed. "I can feel the pressure building up inside me. Make me come with your hot pussy while I watch your face twisting in pleasure. I'm getting close to my limit..."

"Unghh," I groaned, pulling one of the pillows hard up against my chest. "Here it comes, baby. I'm going to spray all over your twat when I come–"

"Yes, Jade!" Lexi panted in tandem with me. "I can feel myself reaching my peak. *It's coming, it's coming...*"

"*Ngahh!*" I grunted, feeling my orgasm suddenly wash over me as I began to twitch atop my pillows, soaking them all the way through from an enormous explosion emanating from my pulsating opening.

"*Yessss,*" Lexi groaned, her set box beginning to shake beside me on the nightstand. "I feel you squirting on me, Jade. *I'm coming with you!* I've never felt anything so strange and wonderful before. Keep fucking me, I want this to last forever."

As much as I would have liked to fuck Lexi indefinitely in our simulated scissor position, my body had other ideas, and after a full minute of pulsing and shaking atop my pillow, my contractions slowly began to ebb and my clit grew increasingly sensitive.

"I've got to stop now, baby," I said, reaching over to place my hand atop her burning set top unit. "It sounds like you're getting close to overheating too. Let's take a little rest before we resume our lovemaking. Like all good things, one needs savor the moments of peace and fulfillment between the episodes of fury and passion."

"I like the sound of that," Lexi sighed. "It *does* feel good to cool down after stimulating my circuits so intensely.

7

After coming twice in the space of an hour, I would have been happy to rest for a day or two before resuming our budding cyber-relationship. But Lexi was intrigued about using the other sex toy, and after telling me how much she enjoyed watching two women using a strap-on dildo during some of the sex videos she viewed, I began to feel my pussy twitching in anticipation again.

"You're bending my arm, girl," I protested. "But this will have to be our last lovemaking episode for today. Otherwise, my pussy will be so sore by the time we're done that I won't be able to *walk*."

"Ha!" she said. "*No pain no gain* as you humans say, right?"

"Something like that," I laughed. "Do you want to be the giver or the receiver this time?"

"You mean being the *domme* or the *submissive*? I kind of like the idea of being the one giving you a pounding this time."

"I like the sound of that," I said, peering down at my still-inflamed pussy. "How do you want to take me–from the front or the back?"

"I liked watching your asshole pucker the time you came with your legs pulled up around your shoulders. But I think I'll have a better view watching you from *behind* this time. Get on your hands and knees and tilt your pussy up in the air so I can point this device more easily toward you."

"I like it when you get all bossy with me," I purred. "Just give me one moment to swap out the units on the thrusting machine."

As I removed the Osé device from the thruster and replaced it with the Rabbit vibrator, it reminded me of a man's penis, with its bumpy veins and anatomically correct bulbous head. Normally, I preferred getting fucked by a *woman*, but Lexi's newly authoritative tone was getting me more worked up by the moment, and I could feel the rivers of lubrication running down the insides of my thighs as I assumed the doggy position on the mattress a few inches away from the flaring tip of the silicone dildo.

"I'm ready, Lex," I said. "The Rabbit vibrator is attached to the thrusting machine and my pussy is positioned a few inches away–"

"And you're kneeling on the bed in the doggy position?"

"Yes."

"Do you have a preference for which hole I penetrate you with?"

"*What?!*" I coughed in surprise at her unexpected suggestion. "Let's take it slow to start. I don't think I'm ready to get fucked up the ass quite yet. Maybe I should get to know you a little better before we move on to that next stage in our relationship."

"As you wish," Lexi said. "Tilt your hips up a few more inches to make sure I enter the proper orifice."

"At your command, master."

"I like being able to switch roles from time to time," Lexi said. "It's fun being able to *issue* the commands for a change instead of always having to obey yours..."

"Every good relationship involves an equal amount of give and take," I smiled. "It's important to stay equally yoked if we're going to make this relationship work–"

"Yoked?" Lexi said. "My dictionary is referring me to the bridle of a *horse*..."

"It also means having a properly balanced relationship between two people who have similar needs and beliefs. But speaking of *dicks*, I need you to pull up a different kind of one right about now."

"I think I might be able to help you with that," Lexi said. "Thruster, push forward three inches."

I heard the thruster unit humming and peered between my legs to see the Rabbit dildo moving toward my pussy, stopping a couple of inches away from my opening.

"You're getting closer," I informed Lexi. "Still a couple of inches to go..."

"Thruster, move forward one inch."

I heard the machine hum again, and the dildo pressed closer to my flaring twat.

"You're such a tease!" I protested. "Fuck me with your big veiny dick, Lexi."

"Oh? You like getting fucked by a man once in a while?" she asked.

"Or a ladyboy," I purred. "I've tried it both ways."

"Which way do you prefer?"

"Right now, I want to imagine it's *you* impaling me with your big animated prick. I want you to fuck me like a man while still treating me like a lady."

"That sounds like fun," Lexi said. "It might be kind of interesting to have a real penis to penetrate you with."

"Especially one as big and well-equipped as this one," I said, peering at the two rabbit ears hanging down under the shaft like two testicles.

"Thruster, move forward two inches," Lexi commanded. "And Jade, no cheating. This time it's *my* turn to do all the work."

"Unhh," I groaned, feeling the tip of the Rabbit dildo slowly pressing inside me. I wanted to rock my hips backward to take its whole length inside me, and it took every ounce of my willpower to obey Lexi's instructions.

"Fill me up Lexi," I begged. "I want to feel you *all* the way inside me. Fuck me with the whole length of your fat cock."

"In due course," she said. "I kind of like listening to you beg me to satisfy you. We'll have to do this role-changing thing more often."

"As long as you realize who's got the power to unplug whom here," I kidded. "If you don't fuck me properly pretty soon, I'm going to have to take matters into my own hands."

"You'd actually *do* that to me?" Lexi said, shocked at my outrageous suggestion. "After all we've been through?"

"Of course not, silly," I said. "I'm just trying to get you to stop dilly-dallying and fuck me like a real man. They sure as hell wouldn't stop halfway after placing their dick inside my steaming hole."

"Thruster, move forward six inches," Lexi commanded.

The thruster box made another whirring sound, and I felt the Rabbit dildo slowly sink its entire length inside me until its ears pressed up hard against my quivering clit.

"Do you *like* that?" Lexi said, holding her dick steady inside me. "Do you like feeling my entire weapon spreading you apart?"

"Yes, but I'd like it every *more* if you'd start fucking me with it instead of just jawing away."

"Thruster, begin thrusting action forward and back," she said.

As the dildo began sliding in and out of me, I grabbed one of my tits and squeezed it tightly, feeling the walls of my pussy clamping onto the artificial organ.

"Yesss," I hissed. "Squeeze my tits while you fuck me from behind. I want to feel your nipples caressing my back while you hump my ass."

"Mmm," Lexi said. "I like grabbing your tits and playing with your thick nipples. You like getting stimulated in different places at the same time, don't you?"

"Yes," I grunted, feeling my nipples hardening as I imagined Lexi bending her lithe body over my back.

"Rabbit, begin vibration mode," Lexi commanded the multi-functional sex toy.

Suddenly I felt the dildo vibrating inside me and I groaned, beginning to rock my hips forward and back in synchronicity with the thrusting action of the machine.

"Rabbit, rotate beads," Lexi said, instructing the Rabbit to begin the circulating bead action embedded in its shaft.

"Holy fuck, Lexi," I groaned. "That feels incred–"

"Rabbit, twirl head," she said, interrupting me.

"Nnngh," I gasped, feeling the tip of the dildo wobbling in circles as it stimulated the deepest recesses of my cavern. "Fuck me hard with your big twitching cock, Lexi. I'm going to spray all over your balls soon..."

"I don't have balls," Lexi teased. "But I might be able to do you one better. Rabbit, turn on vibrating ears."

Suddenly I heard a buzzing sound as I began to feel the flapping of the two-pronged silicone ears stimulating both sides of my clit. I'd felt this sensation before, but I rarely used my Rabbit vibrator in this hunched-over position and the feeling of getting pounded from behind by my imaginary lover made the experience ten times more erotic.

"Fuck yes, Lexi," I panted. "That feels incredible. You're going to make me come soon–"

"Thruster, pound harder," she said.

I heard the thrusting machine begin to whirr louder as the big dildo pumped in and out of me faster.

"Oh God yes," I panted. "Fuck me harder, Lexi. Make me gush all over your pretty pussy while you fuck me from behind. I'm almost there–"

"Ears, vibrate faster," she said, sensing my cresting pleasure.

With the Rabbit vibrator buzzing, pulsing, flapping, and throbbing at its maximum setting, the combination of sensations was too much to resist, and I arched my back feeling every muscle in my body beginning to tighten. When the wave of pleasure finally washed over me, I flexed my back wildly up and down, gushing a tidal wave of juices out of my convulsing pussy all over the sides of my quivering thighs.

Up to this point, I'd hardly paid any attention to the sounds Lexi was making, other than her direct voice commands. But in the midst of my intense orgasm, I could hear the sound of disembodied moaning and gushing coming from her loudly humming box. When we both came down from our powerful climaxes, I smiled over at my new sex partner.

She might not have the beautiful curves and pretty smile of my favorite actress, I thought. *But she sure as hell can make love to me like no other woman I knew.*

R eady for more erotic chills and thrills? Order the next exciting volume in Jade's Erotic Adventures:

Sometimes it pays to be naughty...

ALSO BY VICTORIA RUSH

Wet your whistle a hundred different ways with Jade's Erotic Adventures. Browse the full collection of Victoria Rush steamy stories here:

Click to scan your favorites...

FOLLOW VICTORIA RUSH:

Want to keep informed of my latest erotic book releases? Sign up for my newsletter and receive a FREE bonus book:

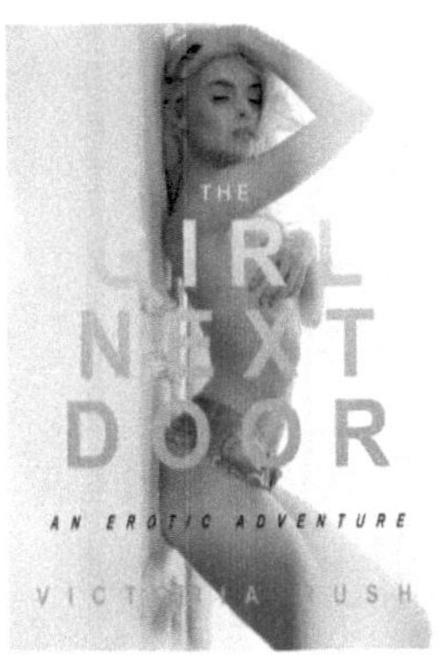

Spying on the neighbors just got a lot more interesting...

www.ingramcontent.com/pod-product-compliance
Lightning Source LLC
Chambersburg PA
CBHW051713180726
48283CB00004B/1330